Story of HĀRUT and MĀRUT

Abdul Waheed

Story'of HĀRUT and MĀRUT

Abdul Waheed

© Abdul Waheed

No copying of this book with out permission

Dedication

This book is dedicated to the memory of my late father Haji Ubairdur Rahman (Munna Bhai) and younger brother Abdul Hameed. May Allah Taala (God) give peace to his soul.

Aamen.

Table of contents

Preface

This book is written on an ancient story Harut and Marut, it is very famous and popular all over the world and described by different names in different texts. Please read this book and inform immediately if you find any deficiency,

Thank you

Date - 27/12/2022

History

"The Quran mentions two angels who teach magic. The names Harut and Marut, however, do not originate from Semitic beliefs but appear to be etymologically related to the two Amesha Spenta of Zoroastrianism, Haurvat and Ameret.

Bürgel, J. Christoph. "Zoroastrianism as viewed in medieval Islamic sources." Muslim Perceptions of Other Religions (1999): 202-212.

His fall from heaven is not mentioned in the Quran; unlike apocalyptic literature, he is described as having been "sent down" by God.

Dye, Guillaume. Early Islam: the sectarian milieu of late Antiquity?. Éditions de l'Université de Bruxelles, 2023.

However, the mufassirs (authorized interpreters of the Qur'an) maintain that they were sent as punishment, and explain the story behind their fall.

The story of the fallen angels teaching magic reflects an early Christian belief. For this reason, some Muslim scholars argue that the story is derived from Judeo-Christian sources (Isra'iliyyat). According to Ansar al-Adl, additional interpretations of this verse came into the tafsir from Judaism or Christianity. The English Quran translator Abdullah Yusuf Ali states that the story developed from Jewish midrashim, particularly Midrash Abakir.

The history of Midrash Abakir, however, does not date earlier than the eleventh century. John C. Reeves concludes that, although the Qur'an integrates previous material, the midrashim is shaped by Muslim beliefs, not vice versa.

Reeves, John C. (2015). Some Parascriptural Dimensions of the Muslim "Tale of Harut wa-Marut". Journal of the American Oriental Society. Western scholars who have studied the "Tale of Harut and Marut" and grappled with its literary analogues have most frequently pointed to the Jewish and Christian parascriptural materials that envelop the enigmatic figure of Enoch and in particular to a curious medieval Jewish aggadic narrative known as the "Midrash of Shemhazai and 'Azael." This unusual tale, extant in at least four Hebrew versions and one Aramaic rendition, requires our attention at this stage, and I accordingly provide here a translation of what is arguably its earliest written registration, in the eleventh-century midrashic compilation Bereshit Rabbati of R. Moshe ha-Darshan.

Careful comparison of the developed narratives of the "Tale of Harut and Marut" and the "Midrash of Shemhazai and cAzael" amid the larger literary corpora within which they are embedded suggests that the Muslim Harut wa-Marut complex both chronologically and literarily precedes the articulated versions of the Jewish "Midrash of Shemhazai and 'Azael," or as Bernhard Heller expressed it over a century ago, "la legende [i.e., the Jewish one] a ete calquee sur celle de Harout et Marout." What is likely the oldest Hebrew form of the story dates from approximately the eleventh century, several hundred years after the bulk of the Muslim evidence.

Similarly, Patricia Crone argues that Jews adopted the Islamic story, especially since stories about fallen angels were considered inauthentic by Rabbinic Judaism.

Crone, Patricia. The Book of Watchers in the Quran. pp. 10–11.

Rejection of the Jewish origin of the story also comes from Muslim scholars. KÜRŞAT Demirci points out that there is no similarity between the story of Harut and Marut and the angels of ancient Jewish lore.] KÜRŞAT DEMİRCİ, "HÂRÛT ve MÂRÛT", TDV İslâm Ansiklopedisi,

Divine Infallibility

"Angels are not generally considered infallible in Islam. Nevertheless, Muslim authors debated how angels could err or advocated for angels in general to be exempt from sin, due to their lack of carnal impulses (Hasan al-Basri, Fakhr al-Din al-Razi, Ibn-Arabi and Ibn Kathir among Sunnis; Sheikh Tusi and Sheikh Tabarsi among Shi'ites).

Mujahid ibn Jabr relates in his version of this story that Harut and Marut's sexuality was in their hearts (qalb), not in their bodies, since as angels they do not have carnal desires. The story also states that a human being prayed for their forgiveness. The human being can be identified with the prophet Idris. Ahmad ibn Hanbal (780-855 A.D.) argued that the infallibility of angels is what caused their transgression in the first place. Because of obedience, they were like Adam They begin to oppose the children of Adam. By doing so, they also question God's judgment, which leads to their downfall. This is in reference to the

Quranic statement in which the angels complain about the creation of Adam.

The bodiless tradition generally allows angels to be wrong. Al-Baydawi claims that "some angels are not infallible, even though infallibility pervades them - just as some humans are infallible, but infallibility pervades them.":545 A commentary in Tafsir al-Baydawi states that the angels' "obedience is their nature, while their disobedience is a burden, while the obedience of humans is a burden and their craving for lust is their nature.:546

Fakhr al-Din al-Razi is an exception and agrees with the Mu'tazilites that angels cannot sin, and that Harut and Marut were only teaching sorcery. He goes further and includes in the six articles of faith that it is not enough to believe in angels, one must also believe in their infallibility. Al-Taftazani (1322 AD - 1390 AD) argues that Angels must not sin, and Harut and Marut were only teaching magic. They would not become unbelievers, but they acknowledged that they could make mistakes and become disobedient. This would be the case with Harut and Marut.

Maturidism also accepts that angels may disobey and face trial. Maturidism generally does not consider sinful Muslims to be unbelievers unless they deny an obligation or prohibition. Abu al-Qasim Ishaq ibn Muhammad al-Maturidi (9th to 10th centuries AD) draws this conclusion based on analogy with the Harut and Marut, who are considered sinners in Islamic tradition but are not unbelievers (kufar).

In the Shia tradition, Hasan al-Askari, the 11th Imam of the Twelver Shia, rejects the violation of Harut and Marut, and considers the angels to be infallible (Ismiyyah).

The Tale of Harut Marut

"Although the Qur'an does not explicitly call this pair of angels fallen, the context suggests it to be true. The story of Harut and Marut (Qisht Harut wa-Marut) is a recurring tale in Qur'anic exegesis (Tabari, Ibn Hanbal, Rumi, Maqdisi, Tha'labi, Kisa'i, Suyuti) to explain the fall of this angelic pair. In brief, this story involves a prologue in heaven resulting in an angelic mission to earth, followed by the corruption of these angels, and consequent punishment by God. Although it bears some resemblance to the story of the Watchers, the most prominent components of this motif are unique to the Islamic tradition and do not reflect Biblical or Second Temple traditions. The story is not about the rebellion of the angels or original sin, but about how difficult it is to be human.

Ibn Kathir attributes at least the details of the story to a fabrication by Ka'b al-Ahbar The story is traced back to a hadith attributed to Muhammad. Tabari narrates the story as follows:"

Harut and Marut (وَمَارُوْت أهَارُوت) are two angels mentioned in the Holy Quran who were sent to Bani Israel to test their faith. Here is the full story about it.

12:26

Background

Bani Israel lived in Egypt for several hundred years where the best magicians lived. Although they left Egypt in 1276 BC during the time of Prophet Musa عليه السلام and migrated to Palestine, they did not give up magic.

When Allah made Prophet Sulayman عليه السلام the king of the jinns, humans and animals in 970 BC, the Bani Israel started claiming that he was a magician.

 They were accusing Allah's Prophet of practicing magic while they themselves were involved in it.

Instead they followed the magic propagated by the devils during Solomon's reign. Solomon never disbelieved, but the devils did

MD 0.100

12:26

Unbelievers - Al-Baqarah 2:102

A test from Allah

At this, Allah decided to test them by sending two of His angels Harut and Marut in human form to Babylon as secret agents.

When Harut and Marut began to show magical miracles to the Bani Israel they were so impressed by them that they wanted to learn it, despite the fact that they knew it was Kufr.

This is similar to what Allah did with the people of Lut when He sent His angels in the form of beautiful boys to test them.

Harut and Marut teaching magic12:27

Before teaching magic to the Bani Israel, Harut and Marut would tell them the religious consequences of this act. They would tell them that Allah did not permit it and that it would endanger their next life.

Harut and Marut never taught anyone without saying, "We are only a test for you, so do not abandon 'your faith'."

Al-Baqarah 2:102

However, they became so fond of their magical arts that they continued to resort to talismans and sorcery.

12:27

Babylon's Favorite Magic

In the same verse of the Holy Quran,

Allah tells us that the people of

Babylon were most interested in

learning magic from Harut and

resolving differences between husband and wife by Marut.

Yet people learned 'magic' which caused a rift even between husband and wife; however their magic could not harm anyone except by the will of Allah. - Al-Baqarah 2:102

Conclusion

Who knows how many angels will still be busy performing their duties among us today!

Therefore, we should be careful when dealing with people12:27

Harut and Marut may be testing us on the orders of Allah.

Another story in Sura 2:102 mentions Babylon by name, but tells of a time when the two angels Harut and Marut taught magic to some people in Babylon and warned them that magic was a sin and that their teaching them magic was a test of faith. A story about Babylon appears more fully in the writings of Yaqut (i, 448 f.) and Lisan al-Arab [ar] (xiii. 72), but without the tower: Mankind was swept together by the winds into the plain that was later called "Babylon," where they were assigned their different languages by God, and then they were scattered again in the same way. In the History of the Prophets and Kings by the 9th-century Muslim theologian al-Tabari, a fuller version is given: Nimrod al-Fida tells the same story, adding that the patriarch Eber (an ancestor of Abraham) was allowed to keep the original language, in this case Hebrew, because he did not want to participate in the building.

Although similar variations of the Biblical narrative of the Tower of Babel exist in Islamic tradition, the central theme of God's separation of humankind on the basis of language is distinct to Islam, according to author Yahia Amrich. He argues that in Islamic belief, God created nations to know each other, not to be separated.

Hadith

Al Imam Muslim ibn al H ajjaj an Naysaburi (may Allah have mercy on him) reported that Imam Muhammad ibn Sirin (may Allah have mercy on him) while talking about the science of hadith said:

"This science is part of religion. So be careful from whom you take your religion. »
[Jāmi' u s s a h i h]

(The Green Dome of the Mosque of the Prophet Muhammad (s a l l a l a li hi wa sallam) in Medina - H ijāz)

'Ilm ul h ā dīth:

* Some definitions of terms used in the science of hadith (Al Jurjanī)

* Regarding the use of weak hadith (An Nawawi)

* Various methods of abrogating the Sunnah by the Sunnah (Ibn ash-Shīkhkhir and An Nawawi)

Comments of an h ā dîth:

* "He who has tasted faith accepts Allah as Lord, Islam as religion and Muhammad (Allah's peace and peace be upon him) as Messenger" (Kishk)

Allah said: "I have divided prayer into two parts, between Me and My servant, and between My servant for what he will ask for. » (An Nawawi)

* "Allah will bring 70,000 people from this ummah to Paradise without any accountability..." (Ar Razi)

* "Allah has a servant [in each place] whom He can devote to you..." (Al Khattar)

* "Allah laughs at two men, one of whom kills the other while both will enter Paradise..." (Al Bukhari, Ibn 'Abd il Barr, Ibn Hajar al 'Asqalani)

* "Allah has stretched out His hand to receive repentance from those who have sinned" (An Nawawi and Al Mazhiri)

* "He who strengthens his ego weakens his religious life, and he who weakens his ego strengthens his religious life" (Ahmad al 'Alawi)

* "Certainly Allah has no need to do anything for Allah, but He has no need to do anything for Allah. From now on, Allah will send a Mujaddid for the Ummah, and this will happen at the arrival of each century" (Shah Waliu Llah)

* Commentary on the Hadith about the most tried men (Ad Darqawi)

* "Do you know how I increased your fame? » (Al Qadi 'Iyad)

Every good deed is an act of charity" (Ibn Battal and An Nawawi)

* "The inhabitant of Paradise will ask his Lord for permission to sow seeds in the gardens of Paradise..." (Al Qastallani)

* "You will see your Lord in the same way as you see the full moon on this night" (Al Qari, Al Maturidi and Dhu Nanun Al Misri)

Hadith: Al Imam Muslim Ibn Al Hajjaj An Naisaburi (may Allah have mercy on him) reported that Imam Muhammad Ibn Sirin (who...
The Light of Islam in the Light of Great Scholars 1433 | 2012.

Harut and Marut in the Bible

The Book of Watchers and the Book of Jubilees

By Hanan Jaber

Whenever a Muslim is asked whether a story or idea is part of their religion, they first refer to the Quran. However, there are some verses in the Quran that do not have much context and need interpreters to explain them. Usually, explanatory writings (tafsir) will contain a variety of stories that go back to the Prophet Muhammad or his companions, and give the context through which the verse was revealed, i.e. when, where or why it was revealed. Modern Muslim readers, who have been taught that the Quran is different from all other Abrahamic books, find it strange how famous Quranic interpreters used Israiliyat (biblical stories that are only found in the Hebrew of the Christian Bible, but not in the Quran) to give context to obscure verses. One such verse that draws attention is verse 2:102. This article compares and contrasts exegetical explanations regarding the angels Harut and Marut mentioned in verse 2:102, and the fallen angels found in the pseudepigraphical works The Book of Jubilees and The Book of Watchers in 1 Enoch. It will be shown that earlier Muslim interpreters were open to using biblical stories to interpret the Qur'an, whereas later scholars became strongly opposed to adding anything that was not contained in codified Islamic texts such as the Qur'an and the hadith literature.

Some Transcendental Dimensions of the Muslim "Story of Harut wa-Marut"

John C. Reeves

2015, Journal of the American Oriental Society 135 (2015): 817-842.

Early commentators and traditionists included Q 2:102, a mystical indication of the complicity of angels in the transmission of esoteric knowledge to mankind, within a rich layer of exegetical lore, often under the title 'The Story of Harut and Marut.' A close study of this verse along with its external narrative embellishments reveals a wealth of structural and contextual motifs that link the 'story' with biblical and liturgical myths about 'fallen angels' and their alleged role in the Judgment. The present paper lists a representative number of these motifs, speculates about their mode of transmission, and provides some guidelines for analyzing the various versions of the 'story' that appear centuries later in medieval Jewish exegetical and mystical literature. Special attention is paid to uncovering the identity of the woman responsible for seducing the angels.

Angels in the Qur'an: Some of Their Roles, Representations and Relationships with the Jinn

Louise Gallorini

2019, Journal of Ethnophilosophical Questions and Global Ethics

This article focuses on the general representation of angels in the Qur'an and their relationship with another category of beings in the Islamic worldview, the jinn. A quick review of the works written about angels in the Islamic world and the appearance of the jinn, as well as an analysis of the Qur'anic verses, will show us that the emergence of Islam was closely linked to the articulation of the place of angels in the worldview of believers. This led to a change in the status and role of the jinn, who were the subject of popular belief in pre-Islamic Arabia, whereby angels played the role of special messengers from the other world, a function that was typical of jinn in pre-Islamic Arabia. The jinn would continue to be an important feature of imagery within the Islamic world, albeit with a modified role.

وبعضها جنى وأنها المعصية محبر ابن عذاب الدنيا وعذاب الاخرة فقال أجدها الصاحد ما تقول
فقال أول عذاب الدنيا سقط وعذاب الاخرة لا يسقط فاحتار اعذاب الدنيا منها النار ذكرهما الله
تعالى بابل هاروت وماروت

وحكى من رآهما قال رأس حسين عظيم جدا قد علقا منكسين ورأسهما كعبها الى ركبتهما
في الحديد ومن رآه احرى ان الله تعالى قال لهما الى ارسل شوا الى النار وليس شيء ومحار رسول
الله لا انزله كالبلاء والاعتلاء والاسرفاء والاسرنا قال كسا لاحجار فلم استد لا يومهما
الذي كلافيه جنى اباجمعها المنعام صحودا انزاء فلما كان امام ادريس على السلم صار الابد
رسالا سندان دعوله اجنى محاور بأله عنهم قال ادريس عليه السلم كيفا العلم بالتجاور شكا
قالا لا ادع الله لا امان راماء فيرو دليل نشجائه وان لم اترامات قموصا ادريس عليه السلم
وصلى ركعتين ودعا الله تعالى ثم لتفس فلم يرها فعلم ان العقوبة وتهطل بما واخذنا الى الارض بالا

هم ملكه شأم اصلاح العالم ودفع المفاسد عنها وقد وكل بكل وم من ارادهما ملكه
بانما الله ودرل ابو احمد عن رسول الله صلى الله وسلم انه فان ... بها ونسرين ملطف

Story'of HĀRUT and MĀRUT

Al-Baqarah 2:102

وَٱتَّبَعُوا۟ مَا تَتْلُوا۟ ٱلشَّيَـٰطِينُ عَلَىٰ مُلْكِ سُلَيْمَـٰنَ
وَمَا كَفَرَ سُلَيْمَـٰنُ وَلَـٰكِنَّ ٱلشَّيَـٰطِينَ كَفَرُوا۟ يُعَلِّمُونَ ٱلنَّاسَ ٱلسِّحْرَ وَمَآ أُنزِلَ عَلَى ٱلْمَلَكَيْنِ
بِبَابِلَ هَـٰرُوتَ وَمَـٰرُوتَ وَمَا يُعَلِّمَانِ مِنْ أَحَدٍ حَتَّىٰ يَقُولَآ إِنَّمَا نَحْنُ فِتْنَةٌ فَلَا تَكْفُرْ فَيَتَعَلَّمُونَ
مِنْهُمَا مَا يُفَرِّقُونَ بِهِ بَيْنَ ٱلْمَرْءِ وَزَوْجِهِ وَمَا هُم بِضَآرِّينَ بِهِ مِنْ أَحَدٍ إِلَّا بِإِذْنِ ٱللَّهِ
وَيَتَعَلَّمُونَ مَا يَضُرُّهُمْ وَلَا يَنفَعُهُمْ وَلَقَدْ عَلِمُوا۟ لَمَنِ ٱشْتَرَىٰهُ مَا لَهُ فِى ٱلْءَاخِرَةِ مِنْ خَلَـٰقٍ
وَلَبِئْسَ مَا شَرَوْا۟ بِهِ أَنفُسَهُمْ لَوْ كَانُوا۟ يَعْلَمُونَ

Azizul-Haqq Al-Umary

And in the kingdom of Solomon, the devils began to follow the lies they were making. While Solomon never committed Kufr (magic), but Kufr was committed by the devils, who were teaching magic to people and they (followed) what the two angels of Babil (city) said; It was revealed to Harut and Marut, while both of them do not teach magic to anyone, until they say that we are only a test, so do not fall into disbelief. Nevertheless, they would learn from both of them that by which they would separate husband and wife, and they could not harm anyone except by Allah's permission, but still they would learn things that were harmful to them. May it be beneficial or not and they knew very well that the one who bought it would have no share in the Hereafter and how bad is the consumption for which they are trading their lives if they only knew!

There are two angels mentioned in Qur'an 2:102, who are said to have been based in Babylon. According to some legends, both of them belonged to the time of Angel Idris. The Qur'an indicates that they were a test for the people and through them the people were tested with sorcery. The story itself is similar to a Jewish legend about the fallen angels Shemzai, Uzza, and Azael. The names Harut and Marut appear to be etymologically related to the two Zoroastrian archangels Horvatat and Ameretat. Horvatat-Ameretat (Pahlavi Hrvad'd 'MWRD'd) appears in Sogdian-language texts as Hrvvat Mravvat. Fallen angel or not.

This folio from the Walters Manuscript W.659 depicts the angels Harut and Marut being hanged as punishment for criticizing the Fall of Adam.

In the Qur'an, the two angels are briefly mentioned as follows:

Mulki Suleman (مُلْكِ سُلَيْمَان,

In the Kingdom of Solomon) they followed what the Shayatis (devils) gave them. Sulayman did not deny, but Shayatin denied, taught men magic and things that descended on two angels in Babylon, Harut and Marut, but neither of them taught anyone until they Said, "We are only a fitna." test), so do not disbelieve." And from these people learn that by which they create separation between a man and his wife, but they cannot harm anyone except by Allah's permission. And they learn that which harms them and does not benefit them. And verily they knew that the purchasers of it (magic) would have no share in the Akhirah (Hereafter). And indeed how bad was that for which they sold themselves, If only they knew!

— Quran, 2:102.

{And when there came to them a messenger from Allah confirming what they had, a group of them, who were given the Scripture, carried the Book of Allah behind their backs. Threw, as if they do not know!}. (Al-Baqarah, 101)

And they followed what the devils gave, that is, all that hinders the remembrance of Allah.

The story of Harut and Marut posed a major problem for the doctrine of infallible angels. Although angels are not necessarily infallible in Islam, many scholars teach that angels are messengers of God without free will, thus incapable of error.

Some Islamic scholars deny that Harut and Marut were angels at all and prefer to regard them as ordinary men rather than angels who learned magic from devils. In Hasan al-Basri's view, it was impossible that the angels would teach sin like magic. This view was also supported by his fellow Tabi'un scholars, Ibn Shihab al-Zuhri, and Qatada Ibn al-Nu'man, who also rejected the notion that angels such as Harut and Marut could commit crimes and commit sins. This view is also shared by modern Salafi-scholars, who reject the notion that Harut and Marut are punished by God.

Others consider Harut and Marut to be angels, but reject their associated story. Hasan ibn Ali ibn Muhammad, the

11th Imam of the Twelver Shia, after being asked about the veracity of the story, rejected the belief that angels could emerge as criminals, as he argued that they should act on their own volition. lack independence and rely only on the will of God. With regard to the Qur'anic statement: "Whatever is in the heavens and the earth belongs to Him, and those who are near Him do not cease, nor tire, of worshiping Him. They glorify [Him] night and day." , and they do it." Not the flag," he reasoned that if Harut and Marut had committed tyranny and injustice, how could they be the representatives or messengers of God on earth?

Ahmad ibn Hanbal (780-855 CE) accepted that Harut and Marut may have been fallen angels and argued that general angelic infallibility is the reason for their crime. Especially because of the disobedience of the angels, they begin to oppose the children of Adam, causing them to fall in the first place, thus the Qur'an's statement about the angels' complaint over the creation of Adam from Harut and Marut. Connect with the relevant rectangle.

Al-Taftazani (1322 AD–1390 AD) said in his 'Aqeed al-Nasafi' that angels can make mistakes unknowingly, but cannot become disbelievers. He confirms that Harut and Marut are in fact angels who taught magic, but never accepted it, therefore did not sin. However, he rejects the angelic nature of Iblis. Harut and Marut are not described as fallen but as repulsed. Al-Damiri (1341–1405) argues that the story of Harut and Marut was unreliable and supports his view from the statements of Hasan al-Basri and Ibn Abbas, although admits that Iblis was once a messenger. He uses this argument to refute the claim that Jurhum was descended from a fallen angel. In Rumi's major work Masnavi, the reader is advised to remember the story of Harut and Marut, and how their self-righteousness led to their demise. On the other hand, Al-Kalbi (737 AD – 819 AD) reconciled the Quranic narrative with earlier non-Islamic sources, mentioning three angels descending to Earth, and giving them names from the third book of Enoch. was given. He explained that one of them returned to heaven, as he repented of his sin, and the other two changed their names on earth to Harut and Marut.

According to the Muslim scholar Ansar Ansar al-Adl, many interpretations of the verse originated from purported Judeo-Christian sources recorded in certain works of Quranic exegesis, known as tafsir. Many stories have circulated about these verses, yet all center around a single core story. Although not explained by the Qur'an itself, Muslim commentators, such as al-Kalbi and al-Thalabi, usually link the reason for their residence to a statement concerning the guards known from 3 Enoch. As in 3 Enoch, the angels complain about the iniquity of humans, after which God offers a test, that the angels may choose three of them to descend to earth, endowed with fleshly desires, and that Prove that they will do better than humans under similar conditions. Accordingly, they choose Aza, Azzaya and Azazel. However, Azazel repented of his decision and God allowed him to return to heaven. The other two angels failed the test and their names were changed to Harut and Marut. They ended up on Earth, introducing humans to illegal witchcraft.

Abdullah Yusuf Ali, the translator of the Quran into English, claims that the source of this story may be the Jewish Midrash:

Jewish tradition in the Midrash contained the story of two angels who asked Allah for permission to come to earth, but succumbed to temptation, and were hanged by their feet in Babylon for punishment. Such stories about fallen angels being punished were also believed by early Christians (see II Peter 2:4, and Epistle of Jude, verse 6).

In contrast, the most recent research in the field of Islamic studies has established that the earliest possible date for the Midrash dealing with the Harut and Marut legend is from the 11th century and thus predates the advent of Islam by more than 400 years. The date is after:

A careful comparison of the "Tale of Harut and Marut" and the developed narratives of the Midrash within the larger literary corpora within which they are embedded suggests that the Muslim Harut va-Marut complex is chronologically and literaryally distinct versions of the Jewish Midrash. is before. The earliest Aramaic version of the story is likely from around the eleventh century, several hundred years after the bulk of the Muslim evidence.

 Similarly, Patricia Crone argues, that the Midrash actually adapted the story from the Muslims, but changed the names to Azazel and Samyza, which were earlier terms for fallen angels in other Jewish scriptures, however, was considered inauthentic by Rabbinic Judaism.

Sadr al-Din al-Shirazi holds that angels are considered mujarradat who are "intrinsically sensible" and free from the limitations of physical existence. A mujarrad, as described by Shirazi, does not necessarily "exist as an abstraction in the mind". It can be a concrete reality in the case of God, angels or intelligence.

Mentioned in Al Quran

Al-Baqarah 2:102

وَٱتَّبَعُوا۟ مَا تَتْلُوا۟ ٱلشَّيَٰطِينُ عَلَىٰ مُلْكِ سُلَيْمَٰنَّ وَمَا كَفَرَ سُلَيْمَٰنُ وَلَٰكِنَّ ٱلشَّيَٰطِينَ كَفَرُوا۟ يُعَلِّمُونَ ٱلنَّاسَ ٱلسِّحْرَ وَمَآ أُنزِلَ عَلَى ٱلْمَلَكَيْنِ بِبَابِلَ هَٰرُوتَ وَمَٰرُوتَّ وَمَا يُعَلِّمَانِ مِنْ أَحَدٍ حَتَّىٰ يَقُولَآ إِنَّمَا نَحْنُ فِتْنَةٌ فَلَا تَكْفُرْ فَيَتَعَلَّمُونَ مِنْهُمَا مَا يُفَرِّقُونَ بِهِ بَيْنَ ٱلْمَرْءِ وَزَوْجِهِۦٓ وَمَا هُم بِضَآرِّينَ بِهِۦ مِنْ أَحَدٍ إِلَّا بِإِذْنِ ٱللَّهِۚ وَيَتَعَلَّمُونَ مَا يَضُرُّهُمْ وَلَا يَنفَعُهُمْ وَلَقَدْ عَلِمُوا۟ لَمَنِ ٱشْتَرَىٰهُ مَا لَهُ فِى ٱلْءَاخِرَةِ مِنْ خَلَٰقٍ وَلَبِئْسَ مَا شَرَوْا۟ بِهِۦٓ أَنفُسَهُمْ لَوْ كَانُوا۟ يَعْلَمُونَ

Sahih International

And they followed [instead] what the devils had recited during the reign of Solomon. It was not Solomon who disbelieved, but the devils disbelieved, teaching people magic and that which was revealed to the two angels at Babylon, Hārūt and Mārūt. But they [i.e., the two angels] do not teach anyone unless they say, "We are a trial, so do not disbelieve [by practicing magic]."[1] And [yet] they learn from them that by which they cause separation between a man and his wife. But they do not harm anyone through it except by permission of Allāh. And they [i.e., people] learn what harms them and does not benefit them. But they [i.e., the Children of Israel] certainly knew that whoever purchased it [i.e., magic] would not have in the Hereafter any share. And wretched is that for which they sold themselves, if they only knew.

In Authentic Tafsir

Tafsir Ibn Kathir (Abridged)

Al-Baqarah 2:102

English - Tafsir ibn kathir

وَاتَّبَعُواْ مَا تَتْلُواْ الشَّيَاطِينُ عَلَى مُلْكِ سُلَيْمَانَ وَمَا كَفَرَ سُلَيْمَانُ وَلَـكِنَّ الشَّيْاطِينَ كَفَرُواْ يُعَلِّمُونَ النَّاسَ السِّحْرَ

They followed what the Shayatin (devils) gave out (falsely of the magic) in the lifetime of Suleiman (Solomon). Suleiman did not disbelieve, but the Shayatin (devils) disbelieved, teaching men magic,

As-Suddi said that Allah's statement,

وَاتَّبَعُواْ مَا تَتْلُواْ الشَّيَاطِينُ عَلَى مُلْكِ سُلَيْمَانَ

(They followed what the Shayatin (devils) gave out (falsely of the magic) in the lifetime of Suleiman) means,

"`During the time of Prophet Suleiman .'Beforehand, the devils used to ascend to heaven and eavesdrop on the conversations of the angels about what will occur on the earth regarding death, other incidents or unseen matters.

They would convey this news to the soothsayers, and the soothsayers would in turn convey the news to the people. The people would believe what the soothsayers told them as being true.

When the soothsayers trusted the devils, the devils started to lie to them and added other words to the true news that they heard, to the extent of adding seventy false words to each true word. The people recorded these words in some books. Soon after, the Children of Israel said that the Jinns know matters of the Unseen.

When Solomon was sent as a Prophet, he collected these books in a box and buried it under his throne; any devil that dared get near the box was burned.

Solomon said, `I will not hear of anyone who says that the devils know the Unseen, but I will cut off his head.'

When Solomon died and the scholars who knew the truth about Solomon perished, there came another generation. To them, the devil materialized in the shape of a human and said to some of the Children of Israel, `Should I lead you to a treasure that you will never be able to use up?'
They said. `Yes.'
He said, `Dig under this throne,' and he went with them and showed them Solomon's throne.

They said to him, `Come closer.'
He said, `No. I will wait for you here, and if you do not find the treasure then kill me.'

They dug and found the buried books, and Satan said to them, `Solomon only controlled the humans, devils and birds with this magic.'

Thereafter, the news that Solomon was a sorcerer spread among the people, and the Children of Israel adopted these books. When Muhammad came, they disputed with him relying on these books. Hence Allah's statement,

وَمَا كَفَرَ سُلَيْمَانُ وَلَـكِنَّ الشَّيَاطِينَ كَفَرُواْ

(Suleiman did not disbelieve, but the Shayatin (devils) disbelieved).

The Story of Harut and Marut, and the Explanation that They were Angels

Allah said,

وَمَا أُنزِلَ عَلَى الْمَلَكَيْنِ بِبَابِلَ هَارُوتَ وَمَارُوتَ

And such things that came down at Babylon to the two angels, Harut and Marut,

There is a difference of opinion regarding this story.

It was said that Al-Qurtubi stated that;

this Ayah denies that anything was sent down to the two angels, he then referred to the Ayah,

وَمَا كَفَرَ سُلَيْمَانُ

(Suleiman did not disbelieve) saying, "The negation applies in both cases.

Allah then said,

وَلَـكِنَّ الشَّيْاطِينَ كَفَرُواْ يُعَلِّمُونَ النَّاسَ السِّحْرَ

وَمَا أُنزِلَ عَلَى الْمَلَكَيْنِ

(But the Shayatin (devils) disbelieved, teaching men magic and such things that came down at Babylon to the two angels).
The Jews claimed that Gabriel and Michael brought magic down to the two angels, but Allah refuted this false claim."

Also, Ibn Jarir reported, that Al-Awfi said that Ibn Abbas said about Allah's statement,

وَمَا أُنزِلَ عَلَى الْمَلَكَيْنِ بِبَابِلَ

(And such things that came down at Babylon to the two angels),

"Allah did not send magic down."

Also, Ibn Jarir narrated that Ar-Rabi bin Anas said about,

وَمَا أُنزِلَ عَلَى الْمَلَكَيْنِ بِبَابِلَ

(And such things that came down to the two angels),

"Allah did not send magic down to the them."

Ibn Jarir commented,

"This is the correct explanation for this Ayah,

وَاتَّبَعُواْ مَا تَتْلُواْ الشَّيَاطِينُ عَلَى مُلْكِ سُلَيْمَانَ

(They followed what the Shayatin (devils) gave out (falsely) in the lifetime of Suleiman) meaning, magic.

However, neither did Solomon disbelieve nor did Allah send magic with the two angels. The devils, on the other hand, disbelieved and taught magic to the people of the Babylon of Harut and Marut."

Ibn Jarir continued;

"If someone asks about explaining this Ayah in this manner, we say that,

وَاتَّبَعُواْ مَا تَتْلُواْ الشَّيَاطِينُ عَلَى مُلْكِ سُلَيْمَانَ

(They followed what the Shayatin (devils) gave out (falsely) in the lifetime of Suleiman) means, magic.

Solomon neither disbelieved nor did Allah send magic with the two angels. However, the devils disbelieved and taught magic to the people in the Babylon of Harut and Marut, meaning Gabriel and Michael, for Jewish sorcerers claimed that Allah sent magic by the words of Gabriel and Michael to Solomon, son of David.

Allah denied this false claim and stated to His Prophet Muhammad that Gabriel and Michael were not sent with magic.

Allah also exonerated Solomon from practicing magic, which the devils taught to the people of Babylon by the hands of two men, Harut and Marut. Hence, Harut and Marut were two ordinary men (not angels or Gabriel or Michael)."

These were the words of At-Tabari, and this explanation is not plausible.

Many among the Salaf, said that;

Harut and Marut were angels who came down from heaven to earth and did what they did as the Ayah stated.

To conform this opinion with the fact that the angels are immune from error, we say that Allah had eternal knowledge what these angels would do, just as He had eternal knowledge that Iblis would do as he did, while Allah refered to him being among the angels,

وَإِذْ قُلْنَا لِلْمَلَائِكَةِ اسْجُدُوا لِإِدَمَ فَسَجَدُوا إِلاَّ إِبْلِيسَ أَبَى

(And (remember) when We said to the angels:"Prostrate yourselves before Adam." And they prostrated except Iblis (Satan), he refused), (20:116), and so forth.

However, what Harut and Marut did was less evil than what Iblis, may Allah curse him, did.

Al-Qurtubi reported this opinion from Ali, Ibn Mas`ud, Ibn Abbas, Ibn Umar, Ka`b Al-Ahbar, As-Suddi and Al-Kalbi.

Learning Magic is Kufr

Allah said,

وَمَا يُعَلِّمَانِ مِنْ أَحَدٍ حَتَّى يَقُولَا إِنَّمَا نَحْنُ فِتْنَةٌ فَلَ تَكْفُرْ

But neither of these two (angels) taught anyone (such things) till they had said, "We are for trial, so disbelieve not (by learning this magic from us).

Abu Jafar Ar-Razi said that Ar-Rabi bin Anas said that Qays bin Abbad said that Ibn Abbas said,

"When someone came to the angels to learn magic, they would discourage him and say to him, `We are only a test, so do not fall into disbelief.'

They had knowledge of what is good and evil and what constitutes belief or disbelief, and they thus knew that magic is a form of disbelief.

When the person who came to learn magic still insisted on learning it, they commanded him to go to such and such place, where if he went, Satan would meet him and teach him magic.

When this man would learn magic, the light (of faith) would depart him, and he would see it shining (and flying away) in the sky. He would then proclaim, `O my sorrow! Woe unto me! What should I do."

Al-Hasan Al-Basri said that this Ayah means,

"The angels were sent with magic, so that the people whom Allah willed would be tried and tested. Allah made them promise that they would not teach anyone until first proclaiming, `We are a test for you, do not fall into disbelief.'"
It was recorded by Ibn Abi Hatim.

Also, Qatadah said,

"Allah took their covenant to not teach anyone magic until they said, `We are a test. Therefore, do not fall in disbelief.'"

Also, As-Suddi said,
"When a man would come to the two angels they would advise him, `Do not fall into disbelief. We are a test. '

When the man would ignore their advice, they would say, `Go to that pile of ashes and urinate on it.'

When he would urinate on the ashes, a light, meaning the light of faith, would depart from him and would shine until it entered heaven. Then something black that appeared to be smoke would descend and enter his ears and the rest of his body, and this is Allah's anger. When he told the angels what happened, they would teach him magic.

So Allah's statement,

وَمَا يُعَلِّمَانِ مِنْ أَحَدٍ حَتَّى يَقُولَا إِنَّمَا نَحْنُ فِتْنَةٌ فَلَ تَكْفُرْ

(But neither of these two (angels) taught anyone (such things) till they had said, "We are for trial, so disbelieve not (by learning this magic from us).

Sunayd said that Hajjaj said that Ibn Jurayj commented on this Ayah (2:102),

"No one dares practice magic except a disbeliever. As for the Fitnah, it involves trials and freedom of choice."

The scholars who stated that learning magic is disbelief relied on this Ayah for evidence. They also mentioned the Hadith that Abu Bakr Al-Bazzar recorded from Abdullah, which states,

مَنْ أَتَى كَاهِنًا أَوْ سَاحِرًا فَصَدَّقَهُ بِمَا يَقُولُ فَقَدْ كَفَر بِمَا أُنْزِلَ عَلَى مُحَمَّدٍصلى الله عليه وسلّم

Whoever came to a soothsayer or a sorcerer and believed in what he said, will have disbelieved in what Allah revealed to Muhammad.

This Hadith has an authentic chain of narration and there are other Hadiths which support it.

Causing a Separation between the Spouses is One of the Effects of Magic

Allah said,

فَيَتَعَلَّمُونَ مِنْهُمَا مَا يُفَرِّقُونَ بِهِ بَيْنَ الْمَرْءِ وَزَوْجِهِ

And from these (angels) people learn that by which they cause separation between man and his wife,

This means, "The people learned magic from Harut and Marut and indulged in evil acts that included separating spouses, even though spouses are close to, and intimately associate with each other. This is the devil's work."

Muslim recorded that Jabir bin Abdullah said that the Messenger of Allah said,

إِنَّ الشَّيْطَانَ لَيَضَعُ عَرْشَهُ عَلَى الْمَاءِ ثُمَّ يَبْعَثُ سَرَايَاهُ فِي النَّاسِ فَأَقْرَبُهُمْ عِنْدَهُ مَنْزِلَةً أَعْظَمُهُمْ عِنْدَهُ فِتْنَةً

وَيَجِيءُ أَحَدُهُمْ فَيَقُولُ مَا زِلْتُ بِفُلَنٍ حَتَّى تَرَكْتُهُ وَهُوَ يَقُولُ كَذَا وَكَذَا

فَيَقُولُ إِبْلِيسُ لَا وَاللهِ مَا صَنَعْتَ شَيْئًا

وَيَجِيءُ أَحَدُهُمْ فَيَقُولُ مَا تَرَكْتُهُ حَتَّى فَرَّقْتُ بَيْنَهُ وَبَيْنَ أَهْلِهِ

قَالَ فَيُقَرِّبُهُ وَيُدْنِيهِ وَيَلْتَزِمُهُ وَيَقُولُ نِعْمَ أَنْتَ

Satan erects his throne on water and sends his emissaries among the people. The closest person to him is the person who causes the most Fitnah.

One of them (a devil) would come to him and would say, `I kept inciting so-and-so, until he said such and such words.'

Iblis says, `No, by Allah, you have not done much.'

Another devil would come to him and would say, `I kept inciting so-and-so, until I separated between him and his wife.'

Satan would draw him closer and embrace him, saying, `Yes, you did well.'

Separation between a man and his wife occurs here because each spouse imagines that the other spouse is ugly or ill-mannered, etc.

Allah's Appointed Term supercedes Everything

Allah said,

وَمَا هُم بِضَارِّينَ بِهِ مِنْ أَحَدٍ إِلاَّ بِإِذْنِ اللَّهِ

But they could not thus harm anyone except by Allah's leave.

Sufyan Ath-Thawri commented,

"Except by Allah's appointed term."

Further, Al-Hasan Al-Basri said that,

"Allah allows magicians to adversely affect whomever He wills and saves whomever He wills from them. Sorcerers never bring harm to anyone except by Allah's leave."

Allah's statement,

وَيَتَعَلَّمُونَ مَا يَضُرُّهُمْ وَلَا يَنفَعُهُمْ

And they learn that which harms them and profits them not.

means, it harms their religion and does not have a benefit compared to its harm.

وَلَقَدْ عَلِمُواْ لَمَنِ اشْتَرَاهُ مَا لَهُ فِي الاِخِرَةِ مِنْ خَلَقٍ

And indeed they knew that the buyers of it (magic) would have no (Khalaq) share in the Hereafter.

meaning, "The Jews who preferred magic over following the Messenger of Allah knew that those who commit the same error shall have no Khalaq in the Hereafter."

Ibn Abbas, Mujahid and As-Suddi stated that;

`no Khalaq' means, `no share.'

Allah then said,

وَلَبِيْسَ

مَا شَرَوْاْ بِهِ أَنفُسَهُمْ لَوْ كَانُواْ يَعْلَمُونَ

وَلَوْ أَنَّهُمْ امَنُواْ واتَّقَوْا لَمَثُوبَةٌ مِّنْ عِندِ اللَّه خَيْرٌ لَّوْ كَانُواْ يَعْلَمُونَ

Tafsir Ibn 'Abbas, trans. Mokrane Guezzou

The Jews left the guidance of all the prophets (And they followed that which the devils falsely related) they acted upon what the devils had written (against the kingdom of Solomon) about the collapse of Solomon's kingdom, and 40 days of sorcery and white magic. (Solomon disbelieved not) did not write this sorcery and white magic; (but the devils disbelieved) did write it, (teaching mankind) the devils taught people, as it is said that the Jews taught people (magic and that which was revealed to the two angels) but the angels were not taught sorcery and white magic; and it is said that this means: they also taught what the angels were inspired with (in Babel, Harut and Marut. Nor did they teach it to anyone) nor did the angels describe anything to anyone (till they had said) at the outset: (We are only a temptation) we have been tried with calling people to this in order that we reduce the intensity of the torment inflicted on ourselves, (therefore disbelieve not) do not learn or act upon it. (And from these two (angels) people learn) without being taught by them (that by which they cause division between man and wife) that by which a man finds excuse to leave his wife; (but they injure thereby) with sorcery and causing rift (no one save by Allah's leave) except through Allah's will and with His knowledge. (And they learn) the devils, the Jews and sorcerers learn from each other (that which harms them) in the Hereafter (and profits them not) in this world or the next. (And surely they do know) this refers to the angels, and it is said that it refers to the Jews in their Book, as it is said that his refers to the devils (that he who trafficketh therein) chooses sorcery and white magic (will have no (happy) portion in the Hereafter) in Paradise; (and surely evil is the price for which they sold their souls) by choosing sorcery for themselves, and the reference here is to the Jews, (if they but knew) but they do not know; and it is said that this means: and they did know this from their own Book.

Royal Aal al-Bayt Institute for Islamic Thought, Amman, Jordan

Asbab Al-Nuzul by Al-Wahidi , trans. Mokrane Guezzou (And follow that which the devils falsely related against the kingdom of Solomon...) [2:102]. Muhammad ibn 'Abd al-'Aziz al-Qantari informed us> Abu'l-Fadl al-Haddadi> Abu Yazid al-Khalidi> Ishaq ibn Ibrahim> Jarir> Husayn ibn 'Abd al-Rahman> 'Imran ibn al-Harith who said: "Once as we were sitting with Ibn 'Abbas when he said: 'The devils used to eavesdrop on heaven. One of them would bring a word of truth from therein, and when he is trusted for telling the truth, he would add to it seventy lies with which he earns the hearts of people. When Solomon came to know about it, he took it and buried it beneath his throne. When he died, a devil stood in the street and said: 'Shall I guide you to Solomon's guarded treasure, the like of which he does not have?' They said: 'Yes, do'. He said: 'It is under his throne; go and unearth it'. They said: 'This is magic'. Different nations then copied it from them. And thus Allah, exalted is He, revealed Solomon's excuse (And follow that which the devils falsely related against the kingdom of Solomon. Solomon disbelieved not.)' ". Said al-Kalbi: "The devils wrote down magic and talismans (niranjiyyat) and attributed them to Asaf ibn Barakhiya. They wrote: 'This is what Asaf ibn Barakhiya has taught the king Solomon' and they buried it in the place where Solomon worshipped without him realizing it. This happened when Solomon was stripped of his kingdom. When Solomon died, they unearthed it from under his place of worship and said to people: 'Solomon left this in your possession so that you learn it'. As for the scholars of the Children of Israel, they said: 'Allah forbid that this be the knowledge of Solomon'. The lowly among people said: 'This is Solomon's knowledge', and therefore sought its knowledge and rejected the scriptures of their prophets. Solomon was later blamed for this and this remained the case until Allah sent Muhammad, Allah bless him and give him peace. Allah revealed Solomon's excuse was revealed in His own words. He showed his innocence from what he was blamed for (And follow that which the devils falsely related against the kingdom of Solomon...)". Sa'id ibn al-'Abbas al-Qurashi informed us in his epistle that al-Fadl ibn Zakariyya informed them> Ahmad ibn Najdah> Sa'id ibn Mansur> 'Itab ibn Bashir> Khusayf who said: "Solomon used to ask any newly grown tree: 'Which disease can you cure?' The tree would say: 'This and that!' When the Carob tree (al-Khurnubah) grew, he asked it: 'What are you for?' it replied: 'I am for the purpose of destroying your sanctuary!' He said: 'Would you really destroy it?' 'Yes', came the reply.

Tafsir al-Jalalayn, trans. Feras Hamza

And they follow wa'ttaba'ū is a supplement to nabadha 'it cast away' what the devils used to relate during the time of Solomon's kingdom in the way of sorcery it is said that they the devils buried these books of sorcery underneath his throne when his kingdom was taken from him; it is also said that they used to listen stealthily and add fabrications to what they heard and then pass it on to the priests who would compile it in books; this would be disseminated and rumours spread that the jinn had knowledge of the Unseen. Solomon gathered these books and buried them. When he died the devils showed people where these books were and the latter brought them out and found that they contained sorcery and said 'Your kingdom was only thanks to what is in here'; they then took to learning them and rejected the Scriptures of their prophets. In order to demonstrate Solomon's innocence and in repudiation of the Jews when they said 'Look at this Muhammad he mentions Solomon as one of the prophets when he was only a sorcerer' God exalted says Solomon disbelieved not that is he did not work magic because he disbelieved but the devils disbelieved teaching the people sorcery this sentence is a circumstantial qualifier referring to the person governing the verb kafarū; and teaching them that which was revealed to the two angels that is the sorcery that they were inspired to perform al-malakayn 'the two angels' a variant reading has al-malikayn 'the two kings' who were in Babylon — a town in lower Iraq — Hārūt and Mārūt here the names are standing in for 'the two angels' or an explication of the latter. Ibn 'Abbās said 'They were two sorcerers who used to teach people magic'; it is also said that they were two angels that had been sent to teach sorcery to people as a trial from God. They taught not any man without them saying by way of counsel 'We are but a temptation a trial from God for people so that He may test them when they are taught it whoever learns it is a disbeliever but whoever renounces it he is a believer; do not disbelieve' by learning it; if this person refused and insisted on learning it they would teach him.

Royal Aal al-Bayt Institute for Islamic Thought, Amman, Jordan

Encyclopaedia Britannica

Hārūt and Mārūt, in Islāmic mythology, two angels who unwittingly became masters of evil. A group of angels, after observing the sins being committed on earth, began to ridicule man's weakness. God declared that they would act no better under the same circumstances and proposed that some angels be sent to earth to see how well they could resist idolatry, murder, fornication, and wine. No sooner did Hārūt and Mārūt, the angels chosen, alight on earth than they were seduced by a beautiful woman. Then, discovering that there was a witness to their sin, they killed him. The angels in heaven were then forced to admit that God was indeed right, whereas the fallen angels faced atonement for their sins either on earth or in hell. Hārūt and Mārūt chose to be punished on earth and were condemned to hang by their feet in a well in Babylonia until the Day of Judgment.

Hārūt and Mārūt are first mentioned in the Qurʾān (2:102) as two angels purveying evil in Babylon, and the legend probably appeared to explain how they happened to be in that position. The story itself parallels a Jewish legend about the fallen angels Shemḥazaī, ʾUzza, and ʾAzaʿel. The names Hārūt and Mārūt appear to be etymologically related to those of Haruvatāt and Ameretāt, Zoroastrian archangels.

Reference- encyclopaedia Britannica

Encyclopaedia Iranica

HĀRUT and MĀRUT, two fallen angels who taught mankind magic in Babylon. They are mentioned once in the Koran (2:96 [2:102]) in a passage admonishing (Jewish) disbelievers who follow the teaching of the Satans (Šayāṭin) at the time of Solomon. "Solomon did not disbelieve, but the satans disbelieved, teaching the people magic [siḥr] and what had been sent down to the two angels in Babel, Hārut and Mārut; they do not teach anyone without first saying: 'We are only a temptation, so do not disbelieve,' so they learn from them means by which they separate man and wife; but they do not injure any one thereby, except by the permission of Allah" (tr. Bell, I, p. 14). The origins of the angels and the nature of their crime are left unexplained, so theologians and Koranic commentators sought to explain the episode by utilizing Talmudic, Syriac, Iranian, and even Greek fables (see below). They came up with various traditions, most comprehensively collected by Ṭabari (Tafsir II, pp. 412 ff; see also Vajda, p. 237), and best studied by Enno Littmann (see bibliography). Side by side with the purely Islamic versions, there also developed a Muslim-Persian rendering which will be treated below.

The Islamic version can be summarized as follows. As mankind multiplied, their sinfulness and debauchery led the angels to complain that God was being too lenient towards them. But God replied that if the angels had been exposed to the same passions and pressures which drove men to commit these carnal sins, they too would not be able to control themselves. The angels volunteered to go down and live on earth like human beings but refrain from committing crimes like them. God made this possible. Two of the purest and noblest of the angels, Hārut and Mārut, descended on earth and for a while led a blameless life until the day they were asked to arbitrate between a beautiful woman (described as a princess from Fārs in some commentaries) and her husband. The two angels became infatuated with her, but she resisted their carnal desires until they granted her a great favor. Some said that she discovered from them the ineffable Name of God that had enabled them to ascend to Heaven at night. By evoking it, she went up and affixed herself to the sky as the planet Venus (Zahrā/Zohra), leaving the sinful angels powerless on earth. Others maintained that she introduced them to wine, whereupon they murdered an innocent passer-by. Angered by all this, God was about to inflict a drastic punishment on the faithless angels, but, at the intercession of a great angel (or a prophet, Edris in some versions), He allowed them to choose between perpetual torment in this world or infernal punishment in the next. They chose the former, and were chained and imprisoned in a well in Babylon. According to Ḥamd-Allāh Mostawfi (cited in Le Strange, Lands, p. 72), the well was "at the summit of the hill." Seekers of forbidden mag-ical arts went there to be instructed by the fallen angels. The Kufan scholar Abu Moḥammad Solaymān b. Meh-rān A'maš (d. 148/765) is quoted as saying that Ḥajjāj ordered the R'as al-Jālut (the exilarch) to guide an inquisitive, pious Muslim to the well, and "they saw the two angels, massive as two mountains, hanging upside down, their head barely above the ground, and chained from the ankle to the knees. In awe the pious man uttered the name of Allah, whereupon the chained ones trembled violently, and their commotion so frightened him that he fainted" (Qazvini, Āṯār al-belād, pp. 305-7).

The development of the story of the fallen angels has been studied by Littmann, Leo Jung (pp. 131-32), Bernard Heller, Josef Horovitz (pp. 146-48), Jean de Menasce, Bernard Bamberger (pp. 114-17), Georges Vajda, and others. They have shown that the theme is ultimately based on the love of the "sons of Elohim" and the daughters of men in Genesis 6:1-4, with the motif of the fallen angels who mastered magic supplemented from the apocryphal books (Jubilees 5:6; Enoch 6-8) and allusions in the New Testament (2 Peter 2:4; Jude 6). The Midrash Abkir, which is rich in old Jewish traditions, calls the guilty angels Shemḥazaie, ʾUzza and ʾAzaʿel, (see also Surābādi, p. 16) and explains how they lost their power by revealing the ineffable Name of God to Naʾamah, the beautiful woman who used it to escape from their unwanted lust and was rewarded for her chastity by God with being allowed to remain in heaven as the planet Venus.

Muslim philologists recognized that Hārut and Mārut were not of Arabic origin (see Jeffery, p. 283 with references), but it was left to Paul Lagarde (pp. 15, 169) to discover that they represented the Avestan Haurvatāt (q.v.)/K̲ordād and Amərətāt/Amurdād (q.v.), two of the Aməša Spəntas (q.v.) who were the guardians of waters and plants respectively (see the detailed study of Darmesteter). He further noted that the 'Zaharā' of the story who became the planet Venus was none other than Anāhid (q.v.) or Bidok̲t (a Nabataean word according to some tafsirs and of Persian origins according to others). The loss of the initial a- in Mārut at such an early date has other parallels. By the time Agathangelos wrote, Armenian had combined the two names Haurvatāt and Ameretāt to form Hauraut-Mauraut, the name for a flower of the hyacinth family (Dumézil; see further Ananikian, p. 62 and Henning, 1965, p. 251[1977, I, p. 626]) "used in popular rites on Ascension Day" (Russell, p. 375). A Manichean glossary pairs Middle Persian ʿmwrd'd hrwd'd with Sogdian hrwwt mrwwt (Henning, 1940, pp. 16, 19 [1977, I, pp. 17, 20]). The Slavonic version of the Book of Enoch names (33.11 B) Arioch and Marioch as guardians of the earth (Littmann, p. 83; Horovitz, p. 147), and the forms once doubted (Jefferey, loc. cit.) are now confirmed by the Aramaic version found at Qumrān (Milik, p. 110).

The demonization of the Iranian Aməša Spəntas in a foreign environment should not come as a surprise. The Qurʾān itself attests a similar case in Surah 27.39, where ʾEfrit "demon" is a transformation of the Avestan genius Āfriti surnamed the dahman "pious," who manifests herself to the righteous when he utters benediction (Gray, Foundations, pp. 130-31; Jeffery, p. 215). There are of course several other parallel analogous examples in a wider context, such as Buddha becoming but "idol" in Persian (Bailey, p. 103).

Side by side with the purely Islamic versions, there also developed a Muslim-Persian rendering, first fully recorded in the so-called Ṭabari's Tafsir in Persian, compiled for the Sāmānid king Manṣur b. Nuḥ in 362/963 (Tarjoma-ye tafsir-e Ṭabari I, pp. 96-97), which draws on material from both Ṭabari's Arabic Commentary on the Koran and his Annals. Other renderings in the early Persian tafsirs tend to add an interesting detail or a new twist to the tale. The Persian variant has not yet received sufficient attention. Indeed, little research has been done on the sources, narrative techniques, and the range of details found in the early Persian tafsirs (see EXEGESIS iii. In Persian), including, for example, Tāj al-tarājem fi tafsir al-Qorʿān le'l-aʿājem of Abu'l-Moẓaffar Šāhfur Es-frāyeni (d. 471/1078), the Tafsir-e Surābādi of Abu Bakr ʿAtiq Nišāburi Surābādi (d. 484/1091), Kašf al-asrār wa ʿoddat al abrār (begun in 520/1126) of Abu'l-Fażl Rašid-al-Din

Meybodi, and Rawż al-jenān of Abu'l-Fotuḥ Rāzi (fl. first half of the 6/12th cent.). Many of the commentaries on this Koranic passage expound on the nature of magic of both licit and illicit categories, and some contain interesting additional details.

The Islamic Persian version of the myth gives the same story but with a divergent outcome: after lusting for the woman and becoming intoxicated with wine and committing murder, Hārut and Mārut were imprisoned inside a well in Mount Damāvand (see DAMĀVAND ii). There they remain suspended by the feet, with tongues stick-ing out because of thirst "although the distance between their mouth and the water amounts only to the thickness of a sword blade. They shall remain so till the end of the world, and whoever desires to learn sorcery goes there and learns magic from them" (Tarjoma-ye tafsir-e Ṭabari, I, pp. 96-97). Damāvand was a favorite haunt of demons or Dīvs (q.v.), and one recalls that a tradition claimed that demonic Zaḥḥāk was taken there by

Frēdun (q.v.) and imprisoned in a well where he would remain until the end of the world. Already the caliph ʾOtmān exiled to Damāvand an Arab who was accused of sorcery (the Arabic text has the Persian word nirang for sorcery), "because that is a land where sorcery is in vogue" (Ṭabari I/6, p. 3033; see further Schwartz, Iran, p. 786). Thus, the link between Damāvand and the fallen angels was natural in Iranian lore. Indeed, by Ṭabari's time, a locality in the Damāvand area had come to be called Bā-bel Donbāwand, "the Babylon of Damāvand," and Suddi located the tormenting place of Hārut and Mārut in "Bā-bel Donbāwand" (Schwarz, loc. cit., with references). Ḥamd-Allāh Mostawfi, who has given a long account of the fallen angel's imprisonment in Babylon, also says (Nozhat al-qolub, ed. Le Strange, p. 37) that Hārut and Mārut are kept in chain in Damāvand. The torment of Hārut and Mārut in the Iranized version of the story is an embellishment derived from classical antiquity. It recalls the myth of Tantalus (Ovid, Metamorphoses 4:458-59; Homer, Odyssey 9:582-92), one of the four legendary figures often associated together (the others being Ixion, Sisyphus, and Tityus) that underwent punishment for various offences. Among Tantalus's offences was that of revealing the secrets of gods to mankind, and he was punished by being forced to stand up perpetually to his neck in a pool of water but unable to quench his thirst, with the water receding whenever he tried to drink.

The "tantalization" of Hārut and Mārut gained wide and lasting currency throughout the Muslim world (Bamberger, pp. 115 ff.). Persian dictionaries define the names as famed sorcerers and as synonyms of sorcery. In the prelude to the story of Bēžan (q.v.) and Manēža, Ferdowsi tells us how in a dark night his beloved fetched him a lamp and prepared a feast of wine, quinces, oranges, and pomegranates and then played the harp so wondrously that the overjoyed poet thought: "you would have said it is Hārut who performs magic (nirang)" (Šāh-nāma, ed. Moscow, V, p. 7; ed. Khaleghi, III, p. 305, n. 2). The reference is of course particularly apt in this context, as

Bēžan was also later imprisoned in a well. Illustrations of Bēžan imprisoned in a well in the hostile land of Turān, and that of Hārut and Mārut hanging upside down in a well in Babylon, formed part of the pictorial cycle of illustrated manuscripts of the Šāh-nāma, in the case of the former, and that of the QesÂsÂasÂ al-anbiyā and ʾAjāʿeb al-makluqāt genre in the case of the two fallen angels (see, for example, Schmitz, fig. 2 from ʾAjāʿeb al-makluqāt, ca. 1050/1640, folio 19). Other Persian poets, most notably NāsÂer-e Ḵosrow, Neẓāmi, and Jalāl-al-Din Rumi, make several allusions to the story in their poetry. In the case of Rumi, he characteristically finds a mystical significance behind the story and in one passage (tr. Nicholson, Book V, lines 182-85) he explains "that the intellect and spirit are imprisoned in clay, like Hārut and Mārut in the pit of Babylon" (R. A. Nicholson, tr., and ed., The Mathnawi of Jalālu'ddin Rumi, translation, III, repr. 1977, p. 14). On the other hand, some Islamic sources were skeptical of the way the story was expanded in the Persian version. Thus, Maqdesi (Badʿ III, pp. 14-15) pours scorn on much of the account and dismisses it as material propagated intentionally by atheists to further their corrupt intentions.

Two later developments of the story of the two angels are worthy of note. The 14th-century Armenian John VI Cantacouzenus cited in an anti-Muslim treatise the legend of Arōt and Marōt, whom God sent to earth "in order to rule well and justly" (Russell, p. 381). Hārut and Mā-rut also make an appearance in English literature from the end of the 18th century onwards as part of a romantic celebration of defiance and rebellion and the interest in the very notion of fallen angels. The pair appears in the poetry of George Croly (1780-1860; see Chew, pp. 201-3) and Thomas Moore (1779-1852). Moore's "The Loves of the Angels," published in 1823 in London, his last long poem and a succès de scandale at the time, deals with the theme in an extensive way. In a more lighthearted and swashbuckling manner, Sir H. Rider Haggard (1856-1925), in The Ivory Child (London, 1916, Chap. IV. Harut and

Marut) alludes to the story in his account of the African magicians, Harut and Marut, who are announced by the butler as "Mr. Hare-root and Mr. Mare-root" and proceed to impress the entire English household with their skill in magic.

Reference- **encyclopaedia Iranica**

My another books

Sr no.	Book
1	World's Major religions, doctrines and sects
2	An introduction to the Holy Qur'an and it's unsolved mysteries
3	How did humans and language originate ?
4	Islam an introduction and sect
5	Sermons of great people
6	Prayer
7	Allah an introduction
8	Is Al khizr still alive today?
9	Story of harut and marut
10	Grief
11	The mysterious story of Al kahf (Ar raqim)

12	Naming of God
<u>**All these books are available in Hindi**</u>** language and other international languages and are also available in e-book for** <u>**free on Google Play**</u> Store.

My personal introduction

My name is Abdul Waheed, my father's name is Late Haji Ubaidur Rahman and mother's name is Jaibunnisa. I have liked scientific ideology since childhood and have a calm nature and attachment to books. Due to which my curiosity interest has been continuously used in new discoveries and information. I got selected in polytechnic while doing BSc, but unfortunately it remained incomplete because father and brother died.

Two words of my father, which are very precious for my life,

<u>first - earn honestly, do not take support of lies,</u>

<u>secondly, respect food and eat as much as you want</u>. That's why the education remained incomplete due to the responsibility of the house, then later getting married. Still did not lose courage and today the book is available in front of you in the form of my thoughts. If any information is left incomplete, please let us know.

Thank you .